New Ghoul
in School

Find out more spooky secrets about

Ghostville
Elementary

Ghostville Elementary™

New Ghoul
in School

by Marcia Thornton Jones
and
Debbie Dadey

illustrated by Jeremy Tugeau

A
LITTLE APPLE
PAPERBACK

SCHOLASTIC INC.
New York Toronto London Auckland Sydney
Mexico City New Delhi Hong Kong Buenos Aires

No part of this publication may be reproduced in whole or in part, stored in a retrieval system, or transmitted in any form or by any means, electronic, mechanical, photocopying, recording, or otherwise, without written permission of the publisher. For information regarding permission, write to Scholastic Inc., Attention: Permissions Department, 557 Broadway, New York, NY 10012.

ISBN 0-439-42439-9

24 23 22 21 20 19 18 17 16 15 14   17 18 19 20

Printed in the U.S.A.   40
First printing, April 2003

To the great kids of Atlanta, Georgia.
Thanks for giving us the Milner Award.
— MTJ and DD

Contents

THE LEGEND

Sleepy Hollow Elementary School
Online Newspaper

This Just In: New kid creeps out the basement class!

Breaking News: A mysterious new boy has joined the third graders in the basement classroom. And he should fit right in — he writes stories that can turn a teacher's hair white with fright!

Maybe the new kid's tales will scare away the secret admirer who's leaving strange gifts in the basement. This reporter is sure the secret admirer is another third grader. No one else at Sleepy Hollow Elementary would dare go down to that haunted museum!

After all, they don't call our school Ghostville Elementary for nothing! Of course, if you ask me, the thought of a secret admirer is spookier than a ghost any day!

Be sure to stay posted for more details.

Your friendly fifth-grade reporter,
Justin Thyme

1
Cobwebs

Deep shadows stretched down the basement steps of Sleepy Hollow Elementary School. Cassidy stared into the darkness and shivered as cold air wrapped around her ankles. "We'll wait for you here," she said.

Nina grabbed Cassidy's arm. "Don't make me go alone," she begged. "It's too scary."

Jeff tapped his foot on the top step. He never could keep his feet still — especially when he'd rather be doing something else. "It's not our fault you forgot your spelling homework."

The three friends had been home for over an hour when Nina remembered the spelling worksheets that still sat in her desk. She had convinced Cassidy and

Jeff to head back to school with her. Now they stood at the top of the hallway steps that led to the basement.

The entire third grade had once been upstairs on a sun-filled floor, but all that changed when Sleepy Hollow became overcrowded. That's when their class was

moved to the basement. It wouldn't have been so bad except for the rumors of ghosts. There had been so many scary stories over the years about ghosts haunting the basement that a lot of kids called their school Ghostville Elementary.

Cassidy, Nina, and Jeff didn't believe in stories. They believed in facts. And the fact was, their basement classroom *was* haunted. They'd seen the ghosts with their very own eyes.

And no matter how many times the ghosts appeared, they still made Nina nervous. Very nervous.

"You know we shouldn't be here after school," Jeff said with a grin. "People might think we like it here."

"I have to get my spelling homework or I won't get a good grade on tomorrow's test," Nina told him. "Please go with me!"

"Quit teasing Nina and let's get this over with," Cassidy said. She led the way down the crumbling steps and into the basement room.

Nina took a big breath before following them. A gust of damp air hit their faces as they made their way along the dim hallway.

Nina brushed a cobweb out of her long black hair. "Where do these creepy things come from?"

Jeff grinned. "Maybe Olivia is raising spiders in the basement," he said. Olivia was Sleepy Hollow's custodian and was known for bringing strange pets to school. Nina shuddered at the very idea. She hated spiders worse than anything else, and Jeff knew it.

Cassidy jabbed an elbow in Jeff's side and shoved him farther down the hall. "Shh," she warned. "Let's try to get out of here without waking up any napping ghosts."

Just before they reached their room, they heard a noise.

"What was that?" Cassidy asked.

Nina turned to run, but Jeff grabbed her arm. He held his finger to his lips as a warning and then peeked through the doorway of their classroom.

It wasn't a ghost at all. It was Olivia. She stood at the back of the room near Jeff's desk, polishing away thick layers of dust and cobwebs from a very old frame. Inside the frame was a picture of a boy sitting under a tree.

Of course, all the pictures in their room looked old. That's because the third graders had made their classroom into a museum. It looked just like a one-room schoolhouse.

Olivia rubbed and rubbed, concentrating on getting every last speck of dust. "If she keeps that up, she'll polish a hole in the glass," Nina whispered.

"She'd better not," Jeff said. "I make up scary stories about that picture. What would I do during social studies if she ruined it?"

When Olivia stood back to admire the

picture, the tools hanging from her tool-belt jingled. Or maybe they jangled.

"There," she said to the picture. "Now you can see all that you've been missing!"

2
The New Boy

The next morning, Nina hurried to the classroom with Cassidy and Jeff close behind her. She didn't want to be late for school. When Nina reached the door, she skidded to a stop. Cassidy and Jeff bumped into her and they all tumbled into the room. A new boy sat in the back corner of the room. His hands were folded neatly on top of his desk. As soon as he saw Nina, Cassidy, and Jeff, the boy smiled and nodded.

"Greetings," he said, standing up. "My name is Edgar."

Edgar wore a faded tie, and his eyes looked big behind his crooked wire-rimmed glasses.

Nina smiled back. "My name is Nina

and these are my friends Cassidy and Jeff. Did you just move here?"

Edgar's smile faded from his face and he looked like he was thinking very hard. Then he smiled again and shrugged. "I think it will be fun to join your class."

"We're glad you're here," Cassidy said politely.

Jeff nodded. "Do you like movies? I like movies. Scary movies. The kind that give you goose bumps!"

Edgar blinked. His eyes looked very big behind his wire-rimmed glasses. "Stories. I enjoy scary stories quite a bit." Then he smiled and winked. "I've even penned a few myself."

"Cool!" Jeff said. "I'm an expert at telling scary stories. Maybe we could trade tales and see which one of us can scare the pants off the other one!"

Edgar stepped back and grabbed his belt. "I do not wish to lose my pants," he said, and he wasn't smiling when he said it.

"You're asking too many questions," Cassidy warned Jeff. "Give Edgar a chance to get used to his new classroom before you scare him with one of your silly stories."

Mr. Morton, their teacher, stopped writing on the board and turned around. He seemed surprised to see Edgar, too. Mr. Morton wiped the chalk dust from his glasses so he could get a better look at the new student. "Welcome to our class," he said, rubbing his hands together. "Now, students, let's get to work. Take out a clean sheet of paper."

"Thank you, sir," Edgar said in a very polite voice.

"Did you hear the new kid?" a boy named Andrew said. Andrew was not known for being polite at all. "He sounds like my grandmother."

"That's enough, Andrew," Mr. Morton said. "I want you all to write three sentences describing your favorite president."

Edgar raised his hand. "I am very good

at writing, but I cannot write a theme without my inkwell, sir," he said.

"Sir, I cannot write without my fingers," Andrew said, hiding his fingers in his fists. Andrew laughed and stuck out his tongue at Edgar.

Carla put her finger to her lips. "Shh, be quiet."

"And be nice," her twin sister, Darla, warned.

Cassidy handed Edgar a brand-new pencil. "Here, you can use my pencil," she said. "The pencil sharpener is in the back of the room."

Edgar seemed to float to the back of the room. When he pushed the pencil into the electric sharpener and heard the motor buzz, he fell against the bookshelf, knocking three lunch boxes to the floor.

"Watch out for those killer sharpeners," Andrew said loud enough for half the class to hear.

Nina glared at Andrew. Then she

handed Edgar a mechanical pencil. "You can borrow my pencil," she said. "It will stay sharp. Just push here if you need more lead."

"Sharper than Nina any day," Andrew said with a laugh. "If you get my *point*."

Nina shook her head. Sometimes Andrew could be such a pain. But when Nina looked in her desk to get her social studies book, something else bothered her. Her crayons had spilled from their box. She carefully put the crayons away and closed the box. The next time she looked in her desk, the crayons were scattered everywhere again. Not only that, but the black crayon had rolled across her math worksheet, leaving an angry mark right down the center.

Nina turned around to see if Andrew was laughing. He was probably behind the whole mess somehow. Cold air slapped her in the face, taking away her breath. She quickly turned around, just in time to see the pages in her book flutter by themselves, losing her place.

"Something is happening to my stuff," Nina said with a whimper.

"Don't worry," Jeff said, making sure nobody else heard him. "It's probably just one of the ghosts."

"I bet it's Ozzy," Cassidy said. Ozzy was their resident ghost bully. He was always playing tricks on them — especially Cassidy.

"Stop it," Nina begged the next time one of her books fell out of her desk all by itself.

"You better behave . . ." Carla warned Nina.

". . . or Mr. Morton will make you stay in for recess," Darla finished.

Even though Carla and Darla had seen the ghosts once, the girls still didn't believe in ghosts. The twins thought they had been dreaming, especially since they hadn't seen anything out of the ordinary since. Nina had learned the hard way that ghosts could decide who got to see and hear them.

When Mr. Morton gave the class a break, Nina hurried out of the room to get a drink from the water fountain. Jeff and Cassidy followed her.

Cassidy patted Nina on the back. "What's wrong, Nina?" Cassidy asked. "You're going to get stuck with a ton of homework if you don't get some classwork done."

Jeff crinkled up his face and grabbed his heart. "Homework! Yuck, there's nothing more horrible."

Nina sighed. "It's not my fault I have a ghost pest."

"It has to be Ozzy," Cassidy said, "but where is the rest of the ghost class hiding? They've been kind of quiet today."

Nina and Jeff knew exactly what Cassidy was talking about. Becky, Nate, Sadie, and Ozzy's dog, Huxley, were other ghosts that lived in their classroom.

"Maybe they escaped upstairs again," Jeff said with a mischievous grin. He looked toward the steps that led to the rest of the building.

Cassidy shuddered. She remembered the last time the ghosts had gotten out of the basement. They made a huge mess and the kids ended up in big trouble. "I don't think they're upstairs," Cassidy said. "I don't hear any screams. Maybe they're just hiding."

"Yeah, maybe," Jeff said. "Anyway, they can't go upstairs unless they take a piece of an old desk with them, and you have the only piece safe at home."

"They can stay hidden forever as far as I'm concerned, because I've had it," Nina said. "If this keeps up, I won't get any of my classwork done." Nina leaned over the fountain and turned on the water.

Water squirted up from the fountain, but it wasn't the kind she wanted to drink. It was green and thick. It bubbled higher and higher until it reached the ceiling.

Nina jumped back and bumped into Cassidy. Cassidy fell against Jeff. All three leaned against the damp wall outside their classroom as the murky water took the shape of a girl.

A ghost girl.

Sadie.

"You!" Nina said more bravely than she felt. "Are you the one who's been

messing with my desk? Would you please leave me alone?"

Sadie wasn't your normal get-in-your-face-and-say-boo kind of ghost. Not like Ozzy. He was an even bigger bully than Andrew. Usually Sadie was too busy moping in a corner to bother anybody.

Sadie's eyes grew round and her mouth formed a big circle. Tears oozed from her eyes and fell into a puddle in the water fountain. "Noooooo!" Sadie moaned. Then she collapsed and disappeared down the drain.

"Now you've done it. Don't you know it's not a good idea to upset a ghost?" Jeff said. He should know. Jeff was an expert when it came to ghosts, thanks to all the scary movies he watched.

"Sadie is always upset," Cassidy pointed out. Which was true. They had never seen Sadie when she wasn't crying or moaning or groaning.

"A sad ghost is one thing," Jeff warned. "But make a ghost mad and we could all be in danger. Grave danger."

3
Missing

Jeff sighed. Studying the presidents was as exciting as watching his toenails grow.

"Who can tell me the name of the president of the United States?" Mr. Morton asked.

The new kid raised his hand high.

Mr. Morton wiped chalk dust from his glasses and peered around the classroom. Edgar was the only one with his hand up. He had been raising his hand all morning. "Edgar?" Mr. Morton said.

Edgar straightened his heavy wire-rimmed glasses and stood beside his chair. "The president of the United States is Grover Cleveland, sir." Edgar grinned wide enough to show a big gap between his two front teeth.

20

Carla and Darla gasped. A few kids giggled. Andrew laughed out loud.

"What's wrong with Edgar?" Nina whispered to Cassidy and Jeff.

"Cleveland was president more than a century ago," Cassidy said. She knew all the presidents because she had spent an entire afternoon looking them up on the Internet for a report.

Jeff shrugged and looked around their classroom for something more interesting than presidents to think about.

He felt like he was in the middle of a history book. All around him were antique desks and even a coal-burning stove the class used to store art supplies. Pictures of kids from more than a century ago hung on the walls. Sometimes Jeff pretended they were scenes from scary movies. His favorite was the one Olivia had cleaned. It showed a boy with heavy wire-rimmed glasses sitting under a tree writing. Jeff imagined the tree limbs coming to life and slowly encircling the boy and his journal.

Jeff looked at the picture while Mr. Morton talked on and on about presidents. Jeff frowned. Something was wrong with the scene. The tree was the same, but . . . the boy was gone. The boy had disappeared!

Jeff blinked three times and looked at the picture. The boy was still missing.

He was about to jab Cassidy in the shoulder to get her attention, but something else beat him to it.

Cassidy wrapped her arms around her waist and shivered as a cold breeze

whipped up the paper from her desk. Jeff caught it for her before it fell to the floor. When he looked back at her, he saw a shadow floating cross-legged in the air above Cassidy's desk.

Ozzy was back.

Once upon a time, Cassidy's desk had belonged to Ozzy. He wasn't very happy about sharing it now. Cassidy stared up at him with wide eyes, but Ozzy wasn't paying attention to her. He looked over her head, straight at Edgar. "What's *he*

23

doing here?" Ozzy mumbled, causing the pencil to roll off Cassidy's desk.

"He's new," Cassidy hissed. "Now, be a nice ghost and go haunt someone else."

Ozzy stuck out his tongue at Edgar. Only when Ozzy stuck out his tongue, it flopped all the way across Cassidy's desk and down to the floor.

"He can't see you," Cassidy whispered. "So why don't you just go away?"

Ozzy folded his arms over his chest and refused to budge. "He chooses not to see," Ozzy said. "I've never liked being ignored."

"You're going to have to get used to it," Cassidy said, "because I'm going to ignore you, too."

That's just what Cassidy did. She didn't even blink when Ozzy stood on his head and twirled like a top.

"Cassidy," Mr. Morton said, "I just asked you a question."

Cassidy had been so busy ignoring Ozzy, she forgot to pay attention to Mr.

Morton. She wished she could tell her teacher just how good she was being, but she knew Mr. Morton wouldn't understand.

Edgar waved his hand. "Perhaps I could help Cassidy with the answer," Edgar said. "Presidents must be aware of what the people want. That is why they travel to the many states."

"Exactly," Mr. Morton said. "Even to Hawaii and Alaska."

"Hawaii?" Edgar asked. "Alaska? They are not states on the map." Edgar pointed to the old map hanging in the front of the room. The map had been there when the class moved to the basement and it was very old.

"Of course they're states," Andrew said with a snort. "Where have you been? Asleep for fifty years?" Then Andrew made loud snoring noises.

By now, Ozzy had stopped spinning. But suddenly, he pointed at Edgar. Ozzy laughed so hard he fell off Cassidy's desk and bounced on the floor.

A few other kids laughed at Edgar, too. Even Cassidy grinned. Not Jeff. He was too busy staring at the picture with the missing boy.

When Mr. Morton finally lined up the class for computer lab, Cassidy and Nina pulled Jeff to the back of the line.

"What is wrong with you?" Nina whispered as her class filed down the hall. "You look sick."

Instead of following the rest of the class, Jeff pulled his two friends around a corner so they could be alone. "Something is wrong," he whispered. "Something is *very* wrong."

"And I know what it is," Cassidy said, tapping her foot on the floor. "We're missing out on computer time. Now, tell us what this is all about and make it quick."

Jeff pointed a shaky finger back toward

their classroom. "The boy," Jeff said. "He's gone."

"What boy?" Nina asked.

Jeff peeked around the corner to make sure the coast was clear. "I'll show you," he said, leading the way back to the classroom. The room was eerily silent as Jeff walked back toward his desk. Then he pointed to the wall where the old picture hung. The same picture that they had seen Olivia dusting. "See," Jeff said. "The boy vanished into thin air!"

Cassidy and Nina looked up at the wall. "The only thing that vanished," Nina said with a giggle, "is your brain."

"She's right," Cassidy said with her hands on her hips. "Nobody is missing from that picture."

Jeff pushed them aside. "It can't be," he said. There in the picture, the boy sat under the tree writing. Just like always.

4
The Boy in the Picture

"I know that boy!" Jeff sputtered and pointed to the picture while Cassidy shook her head.

"This picture is more than one hundred years old," Cassidy said. "There's no way you could know that boy."

Nina leaned over to look. "He does look familiar," she said. "Very familiar."

"He has crooked wire-rimmed glasses," Jeff said with a nod. "And he's wearing clothes just like the new boy."

"What are you talking about?" Cassidy asked, peering at the picture.

"That even looks like the pencil you loaned Edgar this morning," Jeff told Nina, pointing to something sticking out

of the boy's pocket. "That wasn't there
before."

"It had to be there before," Nina said.
"Pictures don't change."

Cassidy looked very closely at the
boy. She rubbed her eyes. "That's just
a kid who looks like Edgar. Maybe it's
his great-great-great-great-granduncle or
something. Now, let's go. We're missing
computer lab."

The three kids hurried into the hallway. Nina shuddered. "Are you guys cold?" she asked.

"More like freezing!" Jeff said. "It's practically the North Pole out here." He rubbed his arms to keep warm.

A wall of cold air stopped them dead in their tracks. The air began to shimmer like a green cloud. Gradually, the cloud took the shape of a boy.

"Oh, no, it's Ozzy again," Cassidy said as a ghost in overalls formed in front of her. No matter how many times it happened, it was always creepy to see a ghost appear before their very eyes.

Next to Ozzy the air moved and thickened until Ozzy's ghost sister, Becky, and their dog, Huxley, became more solid. Becky floated straight at the kids. She didn't stop until her ghost nose was just three inches in front of Cassidy. Cassidy couldn't help but take a giant step backward.

Another spooky shape swirled high in the air like clothes in a dryer. It twisted and turned until it became Nate. Nate didn't have much to say, as usual. Instead, he turned completely upside down so he could look up Jeff's nose.

"Long time, no haunt," Jeff teased.

"It's been a little crowded in the classroom lately," Becky said with a sniff.

"Yeah, we have one too many teachers," Jeff said with a laugh.

Ozzy shook his head. He was serious for a change. "No, too many ghosts."

"We could've told you that a long time ago," Cassidy said.

"It looks like one of you is missing to me," Nina said. "Where's Sadie?"

Huxley barked, but Becky frowned at Nina. "Sadie is sad and it's all your fault!" Becky said as she kicked the wall.

When Becky was mad, she had a habit of kicking things. Unfortunately, when she kicked the wall, her foot disappeared in the bricks.

"My fault?" Nina squeaked.

Becky didn't answer. She was too busy trying to get her foot out of the wall.

"You forgot to concentrate," Ozzy told his sister. The kids had learned that for ghosts to touch things in the real world they had to think very hard. Sometimes Becky forgot.

"Help me, brother." The sound of Becky's voice was high and screechy, like the sound fingernails make on a chalkboard.

"Yip. Yip. Yip." Huxley barked at Becky's foot, adding to the noise in the hall.

Cassidy pulled on Nina's arm. "Come on," Cassidy said. "We don't have time for this. We have to get to the computer lab." The kids dodged the ghosts and ran up the stairs to the rest of the school.

"Why do you think Sadie is sad?" Nina asked. "And why is it my fault?"

"It's not your fault," Cassidy said. "She's been sad for more than one hundred years."

Jeff nodded. "She's always sad," he said with a laugh. "Maybe she doesn't like having to look at your scary face all day."

"Let's forget about ghosts for now," Cassidy told her friends, "and have fun in computer lab."

Cassidy and Jeff started playing their computer games as soon as they got to the room. Cassidy was determined to solve the math puzzles and get to level nine. Not Nina. She looked around for Edgar. She wanted to show him how to play the math games. Nina checked the room. Edgar wasn't there.

"*Pssst.*" Nina asked Carla, "Where's Edgar?"

Carla and Darla, who were sharing

one computer, both shrugged. "Maybe he went home," they whispered together.

"Edgar's not here," Nina whispered to Cassidy and Jeff.

"Shh," Cassidy said. "I'm almost to level five of this game. Maybe Edgar was sent to the principal's office."

"Maybe," Nina said, but she wasn't sure.

"Or maybe," Jeff said softly to himself, "I know where he is."

"Time's up!" Mr. Bailey, the computer teacher, told the kids after about twenty minutes.

Cassidy groaned. Computer class was never long enough, and she had missed half of it thanks to Jeff and Ozzy. As the kids headed back downstairs to their classroom, they once again shivered in the hallway. "Why won't the ghosts go back inside the room?" Jeff wondered out loud to Nina and Cassidy.

"Maybe they lost their hall pass," Cassidy said with a snicker. Actually, she was glad that the ghosts were out of their room. Ozzy had gotten her into plenty of trouble already.

Inside the classroom, Jeff was surprised to see Edgar sitting at his desk in the back corner. "That's weird," Jeff said.

Cassidy shook her head. "I'll show you something weird."

5
Present

"It's a present for Nina," Cassidy said.

Mr. Morton chuckled as the class crowded around Nina. A small package wrapped in brown paper sat on her desk. "It looks like someone has a secret admirer," Mr. Morton said.

"If someone was crazy enough to like Nina, they'd have to keep it a secret," Andrew teased.

"Open the present," Jeff told her. Nina's face was red as she unwrapped the small package.

"Wow!" Darla said.

"It's a necklace!" Carla said.

Nina held up a gold chain with a little heart on the end. "I wish I had one," Cassidy said, and she meant it. The necklace

looked like the one her grandmother wore before she passed away.

"All right, students," Mr. Morton said. "It's time to get to work. Take out your math books and turn to page twenty-four."

The kids found their seats while Nina stared at the necklace. She looked around the room to figure out who could have given her such a nice present. Cassidy was her closest friend, but Cassidy had been upstairs with her. The present was already on her desk when they walked through the door.

Nina shrugged and finished her math lesson in record time. Then she headed back to the reading corner. She opened a book, but all she could think about was the necklace hanging around her neck. Who could have given it to her?

Nina barely noticed Sadie, the sad ghost, as she floated through the door and above the rest of the class. Sadie stopped when she reached the reading corner and perched on top of the bookshelf. She smiled at Nina, but when Nina didn't smile back Sadie moaned.

"Shh," Nina told Sadie. "I'm trying to think."

Sadie flew down to sit beside Nina. "I wonder if Carla left the necklace for me?" Nina said to herself. "Or maybe Darla?"

Sadie flew in front of Nina and did a little dance. Nina didn't notice. She waved Sadie away, but Sadie kept coming back. Nina didn't even notice when Sadie sat down right on top of her book. That's because Nina was too busy looking around the room for her secret admirer.

"All right, students," Mr. Morton announced. "It's time for recess. Let's line up."

Nina slammed the book shut without even looking. She didn't realize that Sadie was trapped inside. Nina tossed the book inside her desk to read later and hurried to line up.

Edgar stood near the end of the line, staring at the door that led to the playground.

"We're lucky we have our own door to go outside," Nina explained to him.

Jeff nodded. "It's a direct escape route to the playground from the horrors of school," he said with a laugh.

"Do you have to make a scary story out of everything?" Cassidy asked Jeff.

Edgar grinned for the first time since

they had lined up. "I like scary stories," he said.

"I know what we can do," Jeff said as the line started moving up the steps. "We can work on a story together."

"Not during recess," Nina said with a groan. "Recess is for soccer and dodgeball. I'm a great soccer player," she told Edgar. "You can be on my team."

Nina followed Jeff and Cassidy out the door. Edgar was right behind Nina.

When they got outside, Nina turned around to show Edgar the way to the soccer field. But all Nina found was air.

Edgar was gone.

6
Secret Admirer

"Where were you?" Nina asked Edgar.

When they came in from recess, Edgar was sitting at his desk, hands folded neatly on top of a pile of papers.

"I looked everywhere for you. You weren't outside." Nina's hands were on her hips and she stared down at Edgar.

"You are mistaken," Edgar said. He blinked his eyes three times and picked up a pencil. "I was outside in the shade. I couldn't find anyone to play with so I wrote in my journal." He tapped his pencil against the papers so hard the pencil lead snapped.

Nina frowned. She was just getting ready to tell Edgar that the playground didn't have any big shade trees when Andrew started teasing her.

"First comes love, then comes marriage." Andrew danced around Nina. "Then comes Nina with the baby carriage."

Nina frowned at Andrew. "In what century did you learn that?"

"Maybe I learned it from your secret admirer," Andrew teased. "Look!"

Nina turned around. She couldn't believe it. There was another present on her desk. What was going on?

Nina was so embarrassed, her face turned red. She grabbed the tiny present and tossed it inside her desk. She was surprised when she heard a soft "ouch."

Nina bent over and peered inside. A small foot was hanging from her reading-corner book. Nina lifted the cover and a very squished Sadie floated out.

"Sorry," Nina said. "Did I do that?"

Sadie sniffled. "You didn't even know I was there."

"I guess I wasn't looking," Nina admitted. "Are you all right?"

Sadie didn't answer and she didn't make any move to leave. Instead, she oozed into the empty spaces of Nina's desk and moaned. Nina sighed. She definitely didn't want to listen to Sadie cry for the rest of the afternoon. Nina looked around. At least no one else could hear.

Nina whispered into her desk, "Please come out, Sadie. I can't do my work with you in my desk."

"This was once my desk, too," Sadie told Nina. "But I will share it with you."

Nina sighed. "It may have been your desk a long, long time ago. But now it belongs to me. Please get out."

"If I must," Sadie said. Teardrops puddled in her eyes. She floated slowly out of the desk just as Edgar passed them.

Sadie took one look at Edgar and screamed. Nina knew that ghosts only let a few people hear them, so she was surprised when Sadie's scream broke the ghost sound barrier. The entire class

turned to look at Nina. Of course, nobody else saw a ghost, except Cassidy
and Jeff.

"Oops," Nina said.

"Nina's scared of her shadow," Andrew
teased. "Or maybe her secret admirer
tried to give her a kiss."

Carla frowned and Darla put her finger to her lips, but Mr. Morton wiped the
chalk dust from his glasses and looked at
Nina.

"Is everything all right?" he asked.

"Um," Nina stammered.

Edgar reached out a hand to Nina's shoulder, but he stopped before touching her. "I believe she saw a spider," he explained.

Nina smiled at Edgar. When he smiled back, Nina had a feeling she had finally figured out who her secret admirer was.

7
Chocolate Hog

"I think I know who my secret admirer is," Nina admitted to Cassidy and Jeff the next morning on the way to school.

"Who?" Cassidy asked.

Jeff swung his backpack around in a circle and said, "Don't you mean who cares?"

Nina ignored Jeff and looked around to make sure no one else could hear. Up ahead she saw Carla and Darla walking to school, but there was no one else in sight. "Edgar is my secret admirer," Nina said.

"What makes you think that?" Cassidy asked.

"It all adds up," Nina said. "Edgar must be sneaking away from the class so he can leave presents on my desk."

"That's disgusting," Jeff said, making a face as if he'd just bitten into a grapefruit.

"I think it's sweet," Cassidy said. "Edgar is trying to make friends at his new school. We should all try to be nicer to him."

"Well, I'm ready if he gives me any more presents," Nina said.

"What are you going to do?" Jeff asked. "Report him to Santa's elves?"

Nina just smiled mysteriously and ran onto the playground. Sure enough, when the kids got into the classroom, there was a new present on her desk.

Nina put the gift into her backpack and handed Edgar something she had brought him from home: a package of homemade chocolate chip cookies.

"My sister and I baked these last night," Nina said. "I hope you like them."

Edgar's eyes got big. "Thank you so much," he said before cramming all the

cookies into his mouth. Edgar concentrated hard on chewing every last crumb before licking his fingers.

"Gheesh," Cassidy said to herself. "You'd think he hadn't eaten in a hundred years."

Jeff grabbed the empty tinfoil wrapper away from Edgar. "You didn't save any for me," Jeff complained.

"So sorry. I should have shared," Edgar said. "I do not know what came over me. I haven't tasted anything so good in years and years and years." Edgar wiped his hands on his clothes. Chocolate stains smeared the front of his starched shirt.

Later, when the class went to the library, Nina decided she would help Edgar find a book. "What happened to Edgar?" Nina asked Cassidy and Jeff. "He was right behind me in the classroom."

"Maybe he's allergic to books," Cassidy said with a laugh.

Jeff pulled his friends aside. "I'll show you where Edgar is. Follow me."

8
Harvey

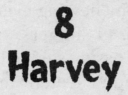

The kids waited until the librarian wasn't looking and ducked out the library door. "Shh," Nina whispered, pulling her friends beside a water fountain. "There's the principal." The kids held their breath until Ms. Finkle clip-clopped her way down to the other end of the hallway and into a classroom.

"Whew," Cassidy said softly, "she didn't see us."

"Let's go," Jeff said. The kids eased down the basement staircase.

"Look out!" Cassidy said as a green glow zoomed close to Nina's head.

"It's just Sadie," Nina said, waving her hand through the air, making the sparkling air swirl and disappear. "She's been acting strange lately — even for a ghost."

Sadie moaned loudly, but the kids hurried away.

In the classroom, Jeff stopped beside the picture of the boy under the tree. "There he is," Jeff said. "Edgar is in the painting!"

Cassidy giggled, but Nina shook her

head. "I think you've watched a few too many scary movies," Nina said.

Jeff tapped on the glass with his finger. "Look at his shirt. Those brown spots weren't there before. They're the chocolate stains from this morning!"

The three kids stared at the boy's shirt. It was definitely stained. "It can't be," Cassidy insisted.

"Yes, it can," Jeff argued. "My dad let me stay up late once to watch this movie where a ghost comes out of a painting. He didn't even know he was a ghost."

"But Edgar doesn't act like the other ghosts," Nina said. "He doesn't mess up the classroom or float through walls or try to scare us."

Jeff nodded. "Edgar may not know he's a ghost."

Cassidy shook her head. "This is crazy. We have to get back to the library before we get in big trouble."

The kids ran out of the classroom and right into Olivia, the janitor.

"Well, what have we here?" Olivia asked, her earrings jingling.

"What have we here?" echoed a parrot perched on Olivia's shoulder.

"Uh," Jeff said quickly, "we're on our way to the library."

"Mmmm," Olivia said. "Usually kids have books with them when they're going to the library."

Nina's face turned red and she quickly changed the subject. "That parrot looks almost bald."

"Back in the picture," the parrot said. "Back in the picture."

Olivia chuckled. "Harvey used to be as pretty as a picture, but then he started missing things from his old life. Poor Harvey. The more he missed the old things, the more nervous he got."

"A nervous bird?" Cassidy asked.

Olivia nodded. "Yes, ma'am. Harvey didn't know what to do so he started preening his feathers until he was almost as bald as a bowling ball."

"Can't you make him stop?" Jeff asked as Harvey pulled a feather out of his wing and let it float to the floor.

"The only thing to do," Olivia said, "is help him see the way things are and to give him some time to adjust. If he doesn't, he'll drive everyone to distraction! We can't have that now, can we?"

9
Ghost Confusion

"How can Edgar be a ghost?" Nina asked as they walked home after school.

"He must have figured out how to go in and out of the picture just like that ghost in the movie I saw," Jeff explained. "Something made him more interested in what was outside the picture."

Cassidy gasped. "Remember when Olivia cleaned the glass? She said something about being able to see better. Maybe she knows."

"Impossible," Jeff said. "No grown-up would let ghosts haunt the basement of Sleepy Hollow."

Nina shuddered. "Being frozen in a picture for years and years must have been awful."

"That's just it," Jeff pointed out. "Edgar

doesn't know he's been in that picture. He probably still thinks he's living in the olden times. He's like Harvey the parrot. Confused."

Nina nodded. "Edgar said he spent the entire recess writing stories. I bet he thinks he's been at recess all these years."

"Cool," Jeff said, tossing his backpack in the air. "One hundred years of recess sounds great to me."

"Well, if he's like Harvey, then we're in trouble," Nina pointed out. "Remember what Olivia said. The more confused Harvey is, the more trouble he causes. What kind of trouble could a confused ghost cause?"

"We definitely don't want to wait and find out," Cassidy said with a nod. "We have to do something, and we'd better do it fast."

"What can we do?" Nina said.

"I don't know," Jeff told her, "but I know someone who does!"

Early the next morning, the kids

sneaked into the basement of Sleepy Hollow, but they didn't go to their classroom. Instead, they tiptoed down the dark hallway. "Ozzy," Cassidy whispered.

"Nate," Jeff called into the shadows.

"Becky?" Nina added.

"Where can they be?" Cassidy asked. "Do you think they're asleep?"

Nina, Cassidy, and Jeff stared down

the long dark hallway. Suddenly, something as cold as ice smashed into the
back of Nina's leg. "Ahhhh!" she screamed.

"Yip! Yip! Yip!" A friendly bark echoed
back.

"Shh," Cassidy said, grabbing Nina's
arm. "It's only Huxley."

Sure enough, the air around Nina's leg
started to glow and turned green. It bub-

bled and swirled until Huxley appeared. He wagged his ghostly tail and nosed Nina's leg again. Nina shivered as she watched the air behind Huxley shimmer and ooze until Ozzy, Nate, Becky, and Huxley stood before her.

"You are early this school morning," Nate said.

"We need to talk," Jeff said. Then he told them about Edgar and how the kids thought he might be a ghost just like them.

"Did you know Edgar?" Cassidy asked. "Before?"

"Of course we knew Edgar," Becky said. She stuck out her lip in such a big frown it covered her chin. "But he didn't like us and I did not care for him, either. So there."

"He was hard to like, that he was," Nate said. "Him with his fancy words and fat books. Always showing off about the things he knew and pointing out the things we didn't."

64

Nina nodded. "He does like to answer questions in class," she said.

"Maybe that's how he was able to figure out a way to be visible all the time," Cassidy said, "and for his body to look more solid."

"He was scary, too," Becky said.

Ozzy put his arm around his little sister. "It was the stories," Ozzy said. "Edgar was forever writing tales that sent our skin to shivering. Claimed he wanted to be the next Edgar Allan Poe."

"Scared us all," Becky added.

"Not me," Ozzy said, puffing out his chest until it was twice the size of the rest of his body.

"So we decided we couldn't be his friends," Becky finished.

"There's nothing wrong with writing scary stories," Jeff said. "What were his stories about?"

"W-well," Nate stammered. "They told about ghosts and goblins and haunts."

Cassidy and Nina smiled. Jeff laughed

out loud. "Then those stories shouldn't be so scary to you now," Jeff decided. "You *are* ghosts!"

Ozzy, Becky, and Nate looked at one another while Huxley chased his tail.

"He does have a point," Nate finally said. "Perhaps there is no longer a reason to fear Edgar."

"I guess not," Becky admitted. "We must explain this to Sadie. She has been so worried."

"Is that why she isn't here?" Nina asked.

Becky pointed a finger right at Nina. "No! Sadie is very upset and it is all thanks to you!"

"What did I do?" Nina sputtered.

"We don't have time to worry about Sadie's hurt feelings right now," Jeff said. "Someone's coming!" The sound of heavy footsteps echoed down the hallway.

Ka-thump. Ka-thump. Ka-thump.

The ghosts immediately faded into the

darkness of the hallway. Jeff, Nina, and Cassidy turned to face the rest of the kids in their class as they filed into their room.

"I can't believe I have a ghost for a secret admirer!" Nina whispered to Cassidy as they followed the other kids. "If Edgar is a ghost, maybe someone else in our school is a ghost, too!"

Nina looked around. What about Carla and Darla? Could they be ghosts? She jumped a mile when Mr. Morton asked for her spelling homework. Could he be a ghost teacher?

Nina groaned when she found another present sitting on top of her desk. She carefully unwrapped the tiny package while the rest of the class watched. Inside was a marble the color of the sunset.

Nina wasn't the only one who thought Edgar was her secret admirer. "Looks like the new kid is losing his marbles," Andrew said with a sneer.

Edgar blinked. He took several short breaths. He looked like he might yell. "I

have lost nothing," Edgar finally said, his voice full of anger. "Nothing!"

"What about Andrew?" Nina whispered to Cassidy. "Could he be a ghost?"

"No," Cassidy said with a determined shake of her head. "Andrew isn't a ghost. He's a monster."

Jeff interrupted them. "Edgar is getting more and more confused and upset. We have to do something before Andrew gets into a battle with the new ghoul in school. We need help. Ghost help!"

10
The Real Story

When the rest of the class left for gym, Nina, Cassidy, and Jeff hid in the back of the classroom. They watched Edgar follow the class to the door. He stopped there as if he didn't know where to go next. He looked upset.

That's when reinforcements arrived. Ghostly reinforcements. Ozzy, Nate, and Becky blew into the room in a gust of air so cold and strong it caused Edgar to stumble back against Mr. Morton's desk. Huxley rushed in after them, barking at Edgar's feet. Sadie was the last to arrive. She took one look at Edgar and sighed. Then she floated to the back corner of the room.

"You?" Edgar cried out. "What are you doing here?"

Jeff, Nina, and Cassidy came out of

hiding before Ozzy could say a word. Jeff pointed to the painting on the wall. The boy in the picture was missing again. "We know your story," Jeff said. "The *real* ghost story."

Ozzy held out his hand toward Edgar. "Welcome to Ghostville Elementary," Ozzy said. "From one ghost to another!"

Edgar blinked. He took several breaths. But this time he didn't look like he was going to yell. He looked ready to cry. "I'm not a ghost," he said. "Ghosts are creepy.

Nobody likes them. I know. I wrote about them all the time."

"That you did," Ozzy said. "And something you never mentioned in all your stories is how much fun it can be!"

"Fun?" Edgar asked.

As proof, Ozzy let his eyes bulge out of his head and all the way down to his chest. "You can do this," Ozzy said.

Edgar smiled. "Really?" he asked. Then he tried it. His eyes bulged and bounced on the floor.

"Watch this," Becky said. She stretched higher and higher until she towered over the rest of the kids.

Edgar laughed. Then he tried it, too. Edgar grew so tall his head smashed against the ceiling.

Nina, Jeff, and Cassidy squeezed against the chalkboard to stay out of the ghosts' way. Nina gasped at every ghost trick, but Jeff laughed out loud.

Edgar tried each ghostly trick that Ozzy, Nate, and Becky showed him. Soon

the ghosts were somersaulting across the room and hopping over desks. Their ghostly laughter bounced off the walls. Huxley ran after them, jumping from desk to desk. Papers fluttered into the air and books tumbled to the floor. Chairs were knocked helter-skelter, and the old map above the blackboard fell to the floor. All the ghosts were showing off — all of them except Sadie. She drooped over her old desk, sniffing as if she were ready to burst into tears. Nobody had time to worry about Sadie, though.

"When Mr. Morton sees this mess he'll think we did it," Nina said.

"We have to make them stop," Cassidy said. "Before the room is destroyed."

Nina summoned up all her courage. "Enough!" she yelled.

Edgar was hanging from the lights. Ozzy was halfway through Mr. Morton's desk. Becky and Sadie were floating across the room. They all froze when Nina yelled.

"There is one more thing you can do as a ghost," Nina said. "You can have ghost friends."

Edgar drifted down from the light until he touched the floor. Suddenly, he looked very, very sad, almost as sad as Sadie. "I never had friends," he said softly. "The other kids, they didn't like me."

"That's because we didn't think *you* liked *us*," Becky told him.

"You have to be a friend to have a friend," Nina pointed out.

Just then, Sadie concentrated with all her might and tugged on Nina's sleeve.

11
Friendship

"Do you really believe what you said about friendship?" Sadie asked.

Nina nodded. "Of course I do."

"Then why won't you be my friend?" Sadie asked. "I said I would share my desk. I tried to keep you company. I even gave you presents."

"You?" Nina squeaked. "You're my secret admirer?"

Sadie nodded sadly, letting giant tears roll down her cheeks and plop to the floor. "You remind me of a friend I once had. A friend who moved away very long ago. I have missed her so. I thought maybe you would be my friend." Sadie looked up hopefully at Nina.

Everyone stared at Nina. Never in her wildest dreams did Nina believe she

would have a ghost as a friend. The idea made shivers scatter across her back and down her arms. But then she looked at Sadie. Even though she was a ghost, she didn't look scary at all. In fact, she looked sad and lonely.

"Of course I'll be your friend," Nina finally said.

"Even if I'm a ghost?" Sadie asked.

Nina took a deep breath. "It doesn't matter what my friends look like," Nina explained, "as long as they're nice."

For the first time since they'd met, Sadie smiled. Her skin turned from gray to a brilliant green. Her eyes sparkled and her hair glowed. "Thank you, Nina. Thank you, friend."

"I'm glad I have friends, too," Edgar said.

"I have a strange feeling that having a ghost for a friend isn't going to be easy," Jeff said.

"Being a friend isn't always easy," Cassidy pointed out.

Sadie smiled. "But it's always worth the effort," she said.

Later, as they lined up to leave for the day, Jeff elbowed Cassidy and Nina. He nodded toward the picture on the wall. It had definitely changed.

Instead of a boy sitting alone, the picture now showed a big hairy dog lying in the shade. Up in the tree, five kids swung from the branches!

Ready for more spooky fun?
Then take a sneak peek at the next

Ghostville Elementary™

#4 Happy Haunting!

Usually Cassidy was good at coming up with plans, but this time she didn't feel like thinking. In fact, she didn't want to have anything to do with the festival. She sighed again. "We could bob for apples," she finally said.

As soon as the words were out of her mouth a cold wind whipped her hair back from her face, as if someone had popped a balloon in front of her nose. Cassidy shivered, hugging herself for warmth.

Nina's lips trembled as she pointed to the air above Cassidy's head. "I think our ghosts are back," Nina said with a shaky voice.

The basement window near the ceiling had whitened with fog. Slowly, a single word appeared on the glass. "NO!" it said.

"It looks like Ozzy doesn't like your idea," Jeff said with a grin. . . .

"Speaking of ghosts," Cassidy whispered. "Look!" The four kids turned to see Ozzy standing above Mr. Morton's head. Actually, Ozzy wasn't standing. He was dancing, and he wasn't alone.

In the air above Mr. Morton, the whole ghost group was dancing. Becky, Sadie, Nate, and Ozzy swung each other around and stomped in the air. Papers flew off the teacher's desk, and a whole container of thumbtacks flew around the room. . . .

Thanks to his dust-covered glasses, Mr. Morton didn't seem to notice.

"They're doing some kind of square dance!" Jeff exclaimed.

Mr. Morton looked at Jeff and smiled. "Square dancing! That's a great idea. Who'd like to do that for the festival?"

"We would!" Carla and Darla called out.

"What's with these ghosts?" Nina asked. "Ozzy can be a stinker, but the rest of them usually let us get our work done."

Jeff snapped his fingers in front of Nina's nose. "I know why our ghosts are bothering us," he said. "Maybe they're unhappy about our families coming to the classroom for the festival."

"Why would having company make ghosts unhappy?" Nina asked.

Jeff pulled his friends close. "I saw something like this in a movie once. A ghost was hiding a secret so terrible the camera wouldn't even show it."

"Are you trying to tell us that Ozzy and his ghost friends are hiding something in the basement?" Nina asked.

Jeff nodded. "And whatever it is, it's something so horrible they don't want anyone to know about it."

"You're crazy," Cassidy told him. "Olivia cleans down here every day. If there was anything to be found, she would know about it."

"The ghosts probably don't understand what the festival is about," Nina added. "If they did, they would be excited. The festival would be the perfect time for them to go into action. Haunting action."

"Shhh," Jeff warned. But he was too late.

Ozzy laughed wickedly from the air behind Cassidy's head.

"What a great idea," Ozzy whispered so only the three friends could hear. "A wonderful, haunting idea!"

About the Authors

Marcia Thornton Jones and Debbie Dadey got into the *spirit* of writing when they worked together at the same school in Lexington, Kentucky. Since then, Debbie has *haunted* several states. She currently *haunts* Ft. Collins, CO, with her three children, two dogs, and husband. Marcia remains in Lexington, KY, where she lives with her husband and two cats. Debbie and Marcia have fun with spooky stories. They have scared themselves silly with *The Adventures of the Bailey School Kids* and *The Bailey City Monsters* series.

MEET
Geronimo Stilton

A MOUSE WITH A NOSE FOR GREAT STORIES

Who is Geronimo Stilton? Why, that's me! I run a newspaper, but my true passion is writing tales of adventure. Here on Mouse Island, my books are all bestsellers! What's that? You've never read one? Well, my books are full of fun. They are whisker-licking-good stories, and that's a promise!

Coming January 2004

Geronimo Stilton
LOST TREASURE OF THE EMERALD EYE

Geronimo Stilton
THE CURSE OF THE CHEESE PYRAMID

Geronimo Stilton
CAT AND MOUSE IN A HAUNTED HOUSE

Geronimo Stilton
I'M TOO FOND OF MY FUR!

www.scholastic.com/kids

SCHOLASTIC

GERSTT